ROUND FISH SQUARE BOWL

Tom Skinner
Illustrated by Mini Goss

NEW FRONTIER PUBLISHING

Have you ever felt as if you *don't quite* fit in?

A bit like a *square* peg

in a *round* hole?

Or a fish out of water,
gasping for air?

Have you ever felt

scared like a little pig?

Slow like a tortoise?

Stubborn as a mule?

Mad as a hatter?

in a china shop?

Ugly like an ugly duckling?

Poor as a church mouse?

But hey!
That's OK!

Because remember
that sometimes
the opposite is true...

The little pig **scares** the wolf away.

The tortoise *beats* the hare.

A **stubborn** mule
can save lives.

The **madder** the merrier.

Bulls can be
very, very, very
co-ordinated.

Ugly ducklings turn into *beautiful* swans.

A mouse can be *rich* with family and friends.

So remember,
be a Square Peg today.
That's what I say!

To Mum.
For your immovable belief that being different was my virtue
rather than my millstone (and thanks for all the library visits). – TS

To my mum, who is often different, in a good way! Thank you. – MG

First published in the UK in 2020
by New Frontier Publishing Europe Ltd
Uncommon, 126 New King's Road, London, SW6 4LZ
www.newfrontierpublishing.co.uk

ISBN: 978-1-912076-09-3
Text copyright © 2006 Tom Skinner
Illustrations copyright © 2006 Mini Goss
The rights of Tom Skinner to be identified as the author and Mini Goss to be identified
as the illustrator of this work have been asserted.
All rights reserved.

Designed by Designed by Ronald Proft,
Cover design by Celeste Hulme

Printed and bound in China
1 3 5 7 9 10 8 6 4 2